TALES OF KING ARTHUR

LANCELOT

written and illustrated by
HUDSON TALBOTT

Books of Wonder   Morrow Junior Books   New York

Long ago, in Europe's dark past, there lived a noble ruler named King Ban, whose kingdom in northern France had come under attack. Hoping to save his realm, Ban stole away with his wife and newborn son to seek the help of his ally King Arthur of Britain.

But the enemy was far closer than Ban had realized. As the fury of battle spread around him, Ban looked back to see his beloved Benwick Castle engulfed in flames. Crushed by this tragic sight, he fell to the ground, dead. The queen rushed to him but then collapsed in grief. Her baby clung to his mother and cried until a pale figure appeared out of the mist on the lake.

"Child of noble blood," whispered the Lady of the Lake, "your destiny rests with me now." Gathering the baby into the folds of her cloak, she stepped onto the surface of the lake and vanished into the mist.

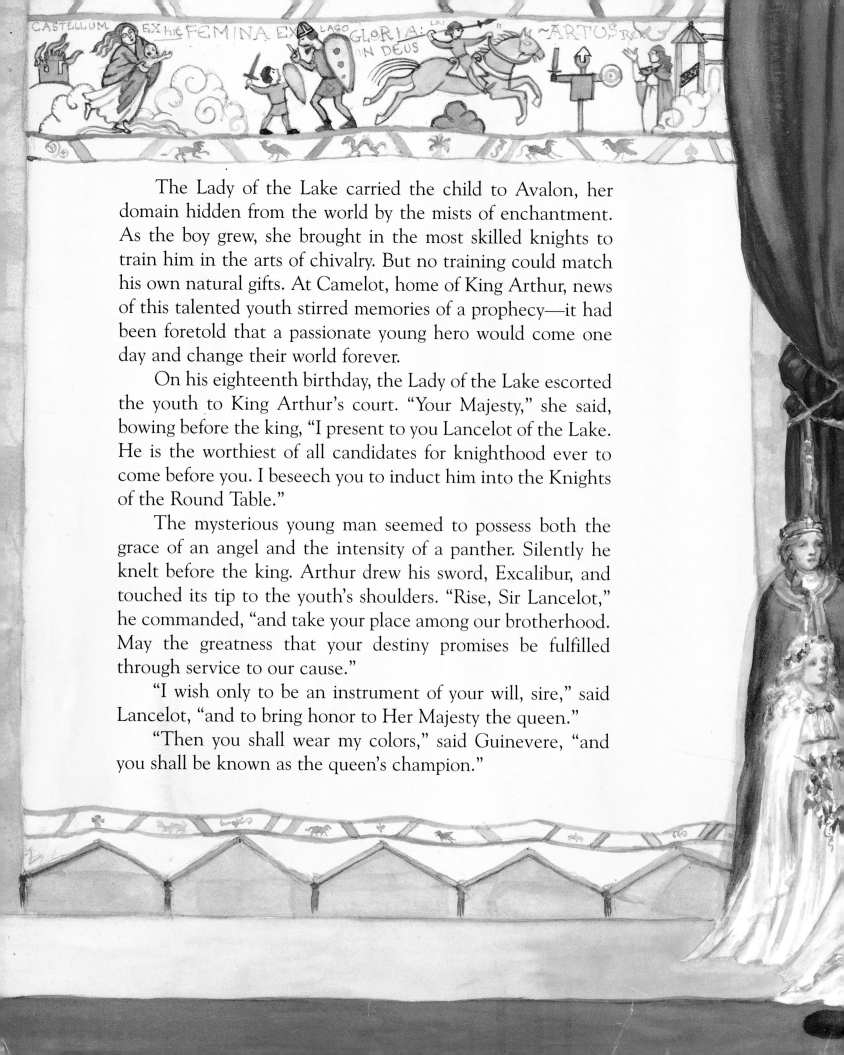

The Lady of the Lake carried the child to Avalon, her domain hidden from the world by the mists of enchantment. As the boy grew, she brought in the most skilled knights to train him in the arts of chivalry. But no training could match his own natural gifts. At Camelot, home of King Arthur, news of this talented youth stirred memories of a prophecy—it had been foretold that a passionate young hero would come one day and change their world forever.

On his eighteenth birthday, the Lady of the Lake escorted the youth to King Arthur's court. "Your Majesty," she said, bowing before the king, "I present to you Lancelot of the Lake. He is the worthiest of all candidates for knighthood ever to come before you. I beseech you to induct him into the Knights of the Round Table."

The mysterious young man seemed to possess both the grace of an angel and the intensity of a panther. Silently he knelt before the king. Arthur drew his sword, Excalibur, and touched its tip to the youth's shoulders. "Rise, Sir Lancelot," he commanded, "and take your place among our brotherhood. May the greatness that your destiny promises be fulfilled through service to our cause."

"I wish only to be an instrument of your will, sire," said Lancelot, "and to bring honor to Her Majesty the queen."

"Then you shall wear my colors," said Guinevere, "and you shall be known as the queen's champion."

The next morning Lancelot set forth to prove himself worthy of his new title. Challenging any knight whom he found causing trouble, he soon was sending a steady stream of defeated opponents back to Arthur for judgment. To Guinevere he sent those who had broken the code of honor regarding women.

Lancelot's quests often took him beyond mere dueling with knights. Once he came upon a town whose young ladies were all being held captive by two giants. Knowing that giants are usually stupid, he devised a plan to outwit them.

"Come meet your fate, you mammoth bags of pig puke!" he yelled from outside their castle.

"'Tis pig puke you'll become when I catch you!" answered one of the giants, rushing out toward the fearless knight. But the brute tripped on a snare that Lancelot had rigged, and he toppled to the ground. Lancelot leaped on the giant and chopped off his head before it had another thought in it. The second giant now thundered forth. Lancelot dodged and weaved until the frustrated oaf threw himself on top of the knight. But as the monstrous body came falling down, Lancelot held his sword straight up and plunged it into the giant's heart.

Exhausted, Lancelot pulled himself from underneath the giant's crushing weight. The maidens ran forth to shower their famous hero with adoration. "I am humbled by your gratitude," said Lancelot, "but my service is in honor of only one lady, our gracious queen, Guinevere."

When spring came, Guinevere invited many of her knights and ladies to go a-maying with her. They planted their maypoles in the lush meadows and danced all day, until the warmth of the afternoon sun and the new May wine gently overtook them.

But in the forest a dark figure was growing ever more alert. Sir Melegrans, the belligerent lord of neighboring lands, had long desired Guinevere. Hearing that Lancelot was away on a quest, he saw his chance to take her for himself. As soon as the queen's knights were dozing, Melegrans and his horsemen charged out of the shadows and surrounded the party.

The maidens' screams sent the sleepy knights scrambling for their swords.

"Stop! I forbid you to fight!" cried Guinevere to her men. "We are outnumbered. He wants only me."

"Thank you for being so reasonable, my lady," said Melegrans. "And now my hospitality awaits your entire company at my castle."

"Your hospitality!" said the queen. "You loathsome . . ." Guinevere stopped when she noticed her smallest page boy hiding under a bush. As she passed him, she dropped her ring to the ground. "Find Lancelot!" she whispered. "And hurry!"

When Lancelot heard of Guinevere's peril, he immediately rode to Melegrans's manor. Enemy archers were waiting for him there and shot his horse full of arrows, but Lancelot was not so easily deterred. Jumping into a passing oxcart, he demanded a ride to the castle.

The castle guards roared with laughter when they saw the mighty Sir Lancelot riding to the rescue on a pile of hay. But he dashed into the castle before Melegrans could stop him.

"Come out, you traitor knight!" Lancelot yelled from the courtyard. "Retrieve your honor on the point of my sword!"

Melegrans had not planned on this. "Take them and be gone!" he called back from his tower, dropping the prison key to the ground. But Lancelot repeated his challenge. He took off his helmet, tossed aside his shield, and demanded to have one hand tied behind his back.

"*Now* fight me!" he shouted.

Melegrans sneaked up behind him and swung his sword at Lancelot's head. Lancelot ducked quickly and Melegrans darted for the door, but Lancelot nimbly blocked his opponent. Their swords clashed as Lancelot went on the attack. With a mighty blow to Melegrans's shoulder, Lancelot brought the coward to the ground.

The queen thanked Lancelot, but his fellow knights turned the rescue into a joke, singing mocking praises to "the Knight of the Cart." Quietly Lancelot returned Guinevere's ring to her and took his leave. They did not see him again for a very long time.

Hoping to put ill feelings behind him, Lancelot wandered in search of new adventures. They were never hard to find, for his fame as a champion of justice attracted them.

After traveling for many days, he noticed a dark tower billowing steam above the horizon. Local villagers told him a young princess had been imprisoned there by a powerful sorceress who was jealous of her beauty. The princess sat day and night in a burning bath, surrounded by fire. According to the village wise woman, there was only one knight in all the world who could free her, for he alone had the goodness and courage to overcome the evil spell.

Lancelot immediately rode to the tower and dismounted. When he struck the doors, they fell off their hinges and great clouds of steam poured forth. Covering his head, he struggled up a winding staircase and kicked open the door.

"Your suffering is ended, my lady," he called to the frightened girl inside.

"Who are you?" she asked faintly.

"I am Lancelot of the Lake," he answered, scooping her into his arms and carrying her out into the cool air.

The maiden was Elaine the Fair, daughter of King Pelles of the mysterious Far Country, whose royal family guarded ancient secrets.

"I know not the way to your land," said Lancelot, "but I would be honored to escort you there, if you lead me."

"And I would be grateful to do so, kind sir," Elaine replied, "for I have another small favor to ask of you when we arrive."

Outside the town of Corbin, in the Far Country, they came to a tomb. Upon it were letters of gold that read: *A panther of king's blood shall come to slay the beast within, and he shall father a lion, and the lion shall surpass all others.*

As Lancelot read these words, the lid of the tomb slid off and a great dragon sprang out before him. The knight tilted his lance and charged forward. His aim was true.

The townsfolk of Corbin were overjoyed to be rid of the demon serpent. They held celebrations for their new hero and begged him to stay. But after several months in the Far Country, Lancelot grew restless and asked to take his leave.

"You would leave us now, when we need you most?" asked King Pelles. He alone understood the prophecy written on the dragon's tomb, and he had waited many years for the right man to fulfill it. "No one could represent us at Astolat better than you."

"Astolat?" asked Lancelot.

"The grandest tournament in many years, my lord," said Elaine, "with all the bravest knights! Will you not do us honor?"

Lancelot knew he would see his fellow Knights of the Round Table there, and their mockery still troubled him. But he missed them all, especially Arthur. The lure of battle finally proved too great for the young warrior, and he decided to

join King Pelles's company in disguise. As he entered the tournament, Elaine called him over and tied a scarf bearing her colors around his arm.

Five hundred knights from all over Britain took to the field that day, but by sunset no one had unseated more opponents than Lady Elaine's champion. Sir Gawain, Sir Lionel, and the other Round Table knights knew that there was only one knight who could fight so brilliantly. They gathered round their brother Lancelot and begged him to return home to Camelot with them.

Lancelot's homecoming was a joyous occasion. Arthur himself ran out to greet him at the gates of Camelot.

"Your Majesty!" said Lancelot, dismounting. He dropped to one knee, but Arthur pulled him up and hugged him.

"At last the wandering spirit returns!" he exclaimed. "We all feared you dead, lad! You must never stay away so long again, no matter how grand the adventures. And you will share those stories with us tonight at the feast the queen and I are preparing for you!"

But the queen's seat was empty at the celebration. Guinevere had heard that Lancelot wore the colors of another lady at the tournament, and she was in a rage.

"How dare you call yourself a knight of the Round Table!" she hissed at him the next day. "You are not who you say you are, and you have dishonored me and all the court! Most of all you have dishonored yourself!"

No sword had ever pierced Lancelot so deeply as Guinevere's words. All at once, his true feelings of love for her flooded his mind, and his face reddened. In a panic, he rushed past Guinevere and leaped out of the window into a thorny patch of briars below.

White with terror, Guinevere peered out the window, fearing the sight of Lancelot's broken and lifeless body. But there was only a trail of blood leading from the briars into the forest.

Lancelot raced through the forest for many days, trying to escape his despair. His love for Guinevere tormented him, and his failure as her champion became unbearable. Madness overtook him. In time, everything he ever knew about himself faded from memory—his beliefs, his identity, even his own name. He lived by eating whatever nuts and berries he could gather and by drinking water from the streams. Like other woodland creatures, he feared all humans

and would dash into the brush if he sensed any nearby. Finally, the friends and kinsmen who searched for him gave up hope.

Sometimes local hunters caught glimpses of the fleeing wildman, and soon tales of horror spread of a half-human creature who haunted the forest. The handsome youth who was once the most admired hero in all of Britain was now the object of fear and scorn. But Lancelot knew nothing but his own sadness.

After some time, a rumor reached Camelot about a wild beast terrorizing the countryside. When the knights organized a hunting party, Arthur seized the chance to look for Lancelot. Arthur alone had kept faith that his friend was still alive.

The king had wandered away from the others when he heard a rustling in the leaves. Bursting out of the underbrush, a gigantic boar charged into Arthur and his horse, knocking them to the ground. But suddenly the boar was fighting for his own life with another strange creature. "A forest goblin?" Arthur questioned, still dazed from the fall. The two crashed into trees and brambles until a savage clubbing brought the boar thudding to the ground.

Now Arthur saw that the "goblin" was human, for he was covered in his own blood. They stared at each other for a long moment.

"Lancelot?" Arthur whispered. Suddenly the hunting horns sounded nearby, and Lancelot vanished.

Fearing that the hunters might catch him, Lancelot fled through the forest day and night. He was desperate to hide, to disappear, to find a place where he would never again be reminded that he, too, was human.

The more he struggled, the more blood he lost. His life was ebbing away with each step, yet he continued to stagger forward. After days and weeks of stumbling blindly, Lancelot finally crawled to a soft patch of grass where he hoped to fall asleep and perhaps never wake up.

It so happened that Elaine the Fair was also seeking a patch of grass that day for a picnic with her ladies-in-waiting. They often came to the lawn near the castle gardens on warm sunny mornings.

"It's a dead man!" shrieked one of the ladies when she saw a body lying near the edge of the forest. "Call the guards! Don't go near!"

But something drew Elaine toward the man, something pulling at her heart. She turned him over and gasped. Lancelot was barely breathing. "We meet again, kind sir," she whispered, wiping his face. "And now it is my turn to save you."

Elaine had her servants bathe Lancelot and lay him in a bed in the highest chamber of the castle. The moment had come to call upon the great secret of her family.

A most sacred and mystical object had been passed down by her ancestors since biblical times, a cup known as the Holy Grail. The Grail had the power of healing and gave infinite joy and peace to those in its presence. Although many would spend their lives in search of it, very few would ever find it. But on this day, by grace and by the compassion of Elaine, it saved Lancelot's life and restored his mind.

The Grail changed all who were in its presence, and so it was with Lancelot. Touched by Elaine's devotion to him, he asked her father for her hand in marriage.

King Pelles bestowed his blessing on the marriage by giving the couple a castle of their own. It stood on an island in a lake, surrounded by gardens and orchards. To Lancelot, it embodied all his hopes for their new life together, and so he named it the Joyous Isle.

When, some months later, news reached Camelot that Lancelot was alive and well in the Far Country, Arthur immediately sent envoys to bring him home. Lancelot was anxious to see his dear friend, but he feared the feelings that might linger between himself and Guinevere.

Elaine found him standing alone one evening, gazing sadly toward Camelot. "It is time to complete your healing," she said softly, "and to present our son to the others who love you. Your fears will fade when you see them again."

Elaine spoke the truth, for the reunion at Camelot was full of warmth and joy and all the good wishes that attend a new-born child.

"What have you called the little fellow?" asked Arthur.

"Galahad, sire," said Lancelot. "It means 'bringer of peace.'"

"Well named, for he has already brought peace to you, lad," said Arthur. "Let us hope that someday he shall help bring it to us all."

AFTERWORD

The tales of King Arthur, Queen Guinevere, and the Knights of the Round Table have beguiled people around the world for centuries. Sir Thomas Malory's classic retelling of these stories was one of the first books ever printed in the English language. Yet though these legends are filled with many gallant heroes, none is as romantic as Sir Lancelot.

Lancelot is first presented as the epitome of the perfect man—strong, graceful, fearless, and the consummate protector of all in distress. And when it comes to his devotion to King Arthur, he is as resolute as any man could hope to be. But then Lancelot discovers his devotion to Queen Guinevere has turned to love, and he falls from chivalrous knight to tragic hero. For how can he remain true to his king and his knightly honor when he is in love with his liege's wife? Tormented by this contradiction, Lancelot flees, not just from Camelot, but from reality as well.

Rescued by the miraculous powers of the Holy Grail, Lancelot is restored to sanity; yet he is never whole again. He will no longer know the serenity and purity of his proud youth. But he does not let that deter him from resuming his role as a champion at King Arthur's court.

This is why Lancelot—more than any other of Arthur's knights—has fascinated readers and listeners around the world for generations. His unwillingness to give up, his determination to do his best despite his inner demons, his strength to carry on in the face of his own disappointment in himself—this is what inspires us. Centuries from now, though many modern heroes will be forgotten, the name of Lancelot and his great deeds will still live on.

—*Peter Glassman*

Watercolors were used for the full-color illustrations.   The text type is 15-point Goudy Old Style.   Copyright © 1999 by Hudson Talbott
Afterword copyright © 1999 by Peter Glassman   All rights reserved. No part of this book may be reproduced or utilized in any form or by any means, electronic or mechanical, including photocopying, recording, or by any information storage and retrieval system, without permission in writing from the Publisher.   Published by William Morrow and Company, Inc., 1350 Avenue of the Americas, New York, NY 10019, www.williammorrow.com
Books of Wonder, 16 West Eighteenth Street, New York, NY 10011   Printed in Singapore at Tien Wah Press.   10 9 8 7 6 5 4 3 2 1
Library of Congress Cataloging-in-Publication Data   Talbott, Hudson.   Lancelot / written and illustrated by Hudson Talbott.   p. cm.—
(Books of wonder) (Tales of King Arthur)   Summary: Lancelot is welcomed into the court of King Arthur as a valiant fighter and later rescues
Queen Guinevere, fights the tournament at Astolat, and pursues other adventures.   ISBN 0-688-14832-8 (trade)—ISBN 0-688-14833-6 (library)
1. Lancelot (Legendary character)—Legends.   2. Arthurian romances—Adaptations.   [1. Lancelot (Legendary character)—Legends.
2. Knights and knighthood—Folklore.   3. Folklore—England.]   I. Title.   II. Series.   III. Series: Talbott, Hudson. Tales of King Arthur.
PZ8.1.Tl33Lan 1999   398.2'0942'02—dc21   98-45248   CIP   AC
Books of Wonder is a registered trademark of Ozma, Inc.